SOPHIE WASHINGTON
CODE ONE

BY

TONYA DUNCAN ELLIS

Other Books by
Tonya Duncan Ellis

Sophie Washington: Queen of the Bee

Sophie Washington: The Snitch

Sophie Washington:
Things You Didn't Know About Sophie

Sophie Washington: The Gamer

Sophie Washington: Hurricane

Sophie Washington: Mission: Costa Rica

Sophie Washington: Secret Santa

Table of Contents

Chapter 1

Game On

"Watch out! Here comes a roll!"

I duck my head and clutch my tray close to my body to avoid getting hit by the hard piece of bread, and then wrinkle my nose at the strong smell of bleach, canned vegetables and mystery meat that fills the cafeteria. The smaller boys, who threw the food at me, crack up laughing, scattering to various tables around the room.

"Sheesh, are those fifth graders immature," I frown and shake a crumb out of my thick ebony braids. My friends and I were definitely not so silly last year.

Lunchtime at Xavier Academy can be a zoo. The teachers sit at tables in the back of the lunchroom, and the kids sit in front near the food line. Since it's a private school, the price of our lunches is included in the money our parents pay. We can go through the line as many times as we want during the thirty minute lunch period, and that sometimes leads to food fights when the teachers aren't looking.

"Let's sit at that table over there." My best friend Chloe points to some seats near our other classmates, Nathan Jones, Toby Johnson and Carlton Gibson. Chloe and I usually sit with the other members of our cheerleading squad, Valentina Martinez and Mariama Asante, but I don't see them.

"Hey, guys, what's up?" Chloe asks, then flashes her too-white-to-be-true smile and shakes her glossy, black curls. She's one of the prettiest girls in our sixth grade class, and also one of the most popular. Chloe gets all the attention from the boys, especially Toby, who has followed her around like my dog Bertram chasing a tennis ball, since he transferred to our school last year. Chloe won't admit it, but she kind of likes him, too. Kids in our class call them ToChlo behind their backs.

"Hey, ladies," Toby grins back and shows his dimple. I remember when his smile made my day go from gray to rainbow bright. I had a major crush on Toby when he came to Xavier and went through all kinds of changes to get his attention. I'm embarrassed thinking about how I acted like I love basketball, which I can't stand, because he is a star player on our school's team, and how I even swiped a cell phone from one of my little brother's friends so I could call Toby. I found out he didn't really care about any of that stuff and liked me for myself. We aren't a couple or anything, but I'm glad we're friends.

"Whatcha reading?" I point at pieces of paper on the table that the boys are staring at like they're Willy Wonka's golden tickets.

"An invitation for teams to sign up for the new computer coding club," answers Nathan, pushing his dark-rimmed glasses up on his nose. "Xavier is having a coding competition to see who can make the best computer app."

"What's coding?" I ask.

"A special language that computer programmers use to tell the computer what to do," Nathan explains. "like show a video, or start a game."

"We're thinking about making an app that's similar to the video game, Fortify," says Toby. "The grand prize is two hundred dollars, and it's split between all the team members. I want some new basketball shoes, and my dad says I have to come up with half the money myself, so this will be a quick way to get it."

"Count us in!" enthuses Chloe. "We could always use some extra cash for trips to the mall."

"Yeah, that sounds like fun," I add.

"Wait a minute, ladies," says Nathan. "Coding isn't as easy as turning a cartwheel. We really want to win."

"What's that supposed to mean?" asks Chloe, putting her hands on her hips. "You don't think you could win with us on the team?"

"I-I didn't say that," he stammers. "It's just with your...umm...disability and all...and all the time you have to practice for cheerleading, I wonder if you could really help us."

Now he's done it. I can almost see the steam coming out of Chloe's curls. My best friend has dyslexia, a condition that makes her see numbers and letters differently. Because of it, she takes longer to read and do math than other kids and is in some special classes. She gets very angry when people make fun of her about it, or act like she's not smart.

"If you're so worried about us being in cheer why would you pick Toby for the team?" Chloe counters. "He practices his basketball just as much as we practice for cheerleading, and we're all at the same games."

"Toby is a level one Fortify player," Nathan says. "He knows everything about the game, so he can help us write a plan for how the app should work."

"Oooo, I guess we should bow down to the expert," says Chloe.

"My eight-year-old brother Cole plays Fortify," I pipe in. "I'm sure it's not too hard to figure out."

"Yeah, you guys just don't want us," Chloe frowns.

"Nobody's trying to keep you girls from being on the team." Carlton holds his palms up to keep the peace. "It's just that we've asked a couple other guys to be on our team already, so we don't have room for anyone else."

"Exactly. We'd love to have the extra 'brain power,' but our group is full," Nathan agrees. "In fact, I wish I could make an app to clone myself. Then I'd have another person to do my school assignments while I'm working on this."

"Why'd we want to have two of you?" says Chloe. "There are enough jerks running around this school. Come on, Sophie! Since their group is so 'crowded,' let's find a table where there is enough space for us."

She turns on her heels and moves toward another table, and I follow.

"Chloe, hold up! Don't be like that!" Toby calls. She doesn't look back.

"Let her go, man," says Nathan, "It's not worth it." They turn back to the flyers.

"The nerve of those boys!" Chloe huffs as we sit down at a table in a corner of the room. "I can't believe they think we're not smart enough to help them win the competition."

I shake my head and smooth my uniform skirt. I am especially surprised at Nathan, since I beat him in both the school and regional spelling bees last year. "They think we're dumb just because we are cheerleaders and because we're girls."

"Well, we'll show them!" Chloe yanks a coding club flyer off the cafeteria wall. "Let's sign up for the competition and beat the pants off them!"

"Yeah, they'll wish that they begged us to be on their team!" I agree.

We high five, and then start reviewing the contest rules as we eat our sandwiches. The coding club meeting is tomorrow afternoon in the school computer lab. I can't wait to see Nathan's and Toby's faces when we show up with our own winning team.

It's game on!

Chapter 2

Code One

"The first thing we need to do is come up with a name." Chloe holds her sparkly, hot pink glitter pen with the silk flower on the top, at attention. "Anybody have any ideas?"

It's our free period class time at the end of the school day, and we are sitting at a back table in the library with Valentina and Mariama.

"How about las reinas de las computadoras?" interjects Valentina. Her family immigrated to America from Mexico, and she speaks Spanish at home and with us sometimes. Valentina lives with her grandmother, or abuela, as she calls her in Spanish, and her little brother Hector.

"Rainy de la who? What's that supposed to mean?" questions Mariama, eyebrows raised.

"The computer queens," Valentina answers. "We need to let them know we mean business."

"I like it," Chloe shakes her head in agreement, "but we might want to choose a name the other teams can understand without getting their Spanish books out."

Valentina was even madder than Chloe was when she found out how the boys kept us off their team. She couldn't wait to sign up for the coding competition.

"Like mi abuela always tells me, anything boys can do, girls can definitely do better!" she said, shaking her shoulder length, silky black hair and writing her name on the team list with a flourish.

Mariama is actually interested in computers, and said she had been meaning to ask us about putting a team together when she saw the flyer the other day, so she is also excited about the coding club. It doesn't surprise me because, though we all get good grades, she's the most studious one in our group.

"Let's call our team Code One," I suggest. "We'll be coding, and we want our project to be number one, or first place, right?"

"I thought Code One means there is an emergency?" Mariama responds.

"Well, it will be an emergency for Nathan and Toby when we beat their team, so I say let's use it!" Chloe enthuses.

"Code One it is!" Valentina pumps her fist in the air like she's at a pep rally.

"Girls, please!" Mrs. Granger, the school librarian, frowns at us over her horn-rimmed glasses and makes a shushing motion with her hands.

"The competition rules say that there needs to be five members on each team," whispers Mariama. "We only have four. Who else could we add?"

"It definitely should be another girl," says Chloe. "I want Nathan Jones to get whooped by someone with a skirt to show him that we aren't all dumbbells just because we wear hair bows."

"Now he didn't say that, Chloe." I surprise myself by jumping to Nathan's defense.

"Well he may as well have," Chloe retorts. "You saw how he was coming up with any excuse he could to keep us off the team."

"What about asking Rani Patel to join our team?" asks Valentina. "She always gets the best grades in our advanced math class."

"You mean that girl who tripped over my shoes in assembly last week?" asks Mariama.

"Yeah, she also bumped into me in the lunch line yesterday," says Chloe. "Rani always has her nose in a book and doesn't pay attention to where she's going."

"All that reading must pay off because Rani won first place for math in the academic meet last spring," I add.

"She sounds perfect!" enthuses Valentina. "Can you ask her to join Code One in the carpool line after school, Sophie? She stands near where you come out for dismissal." I nod my head yes.

"Looks like we are on our way!"

Chloe gets out of her chair in a cheer stance.

"Let's hear it for Code One, ladies! All for one and one for all!"

"All right, Code One!" Valentina cheers and kicks up her leg.

"Shhhh!" Mrs. Granger frowns at our table again, and other kids start laughing.

We put our heads down, giggling, and continue to make plans for our team.

Chapter 3

Meeting Rani

For the most part, I enjoy being a private school student. Our classes are smaller, we get lots of help from our teachers, and I like all my friends. But I do wish I rode the bus every day like kids in public school. It would be so much fun to wait at the bus stop and ride on a yellow school bus with kids my age. My mother drives me to and from school every day and my only company is my eight-year-old little brother, whose idea of a great conversation is talking about what character he destroyed in his latest video game.

As soon as the school bell rings, I rush to the car pool waiting area. My mother is usually on time, and I don't want to miss a chance to speak with Rani. I've said hi to her a few times, but I wouldn't really consider her a friend. She doesn't hang out much or talk to many people at lunch or recess. Her family is from India, and she is very focused on her grades. Rani's parents make her study twenty-four-seven; any grade less than an "A" means big trouble. One time, I overheard Rani say her older brother, Aryan, couldn't watch TV for two weeks because he got a "B" on his report card! And I thought my parents were strict. It's a good thing she wasn't in the spelling bee last year when I won because I'm sure she would have given me a run for my money.

"Hey, Rani!" I bump my way through the throng of kids with my backpack to get close to my potential teammate.

"Oh, hi, Sophie." Rani looks up from the book she's reading in surprise and almost knocks over the girl beside her with her backpack. "Oops, sorry!" she says.

Rani's eyes are an unusual green, though her skin is the golden brown color you normally see in people from India. She sometimes wears a thick, gold necklace with her uniform polo shirt and almost always has her hair in a ponytail. Houston, the city we live in, is what my father calls a real "melting pot." People who live here come from all over the world. My friend Mariama was born in Nigeria in Africa, Valentina's family comes from Mexico, and my brother Cole has friends in our neighborhood whose mother is from Vietnam.

I sway back and forth with my bookbag at my side. I'm kind of nervous. What if Rani turns me down? Seeing her thumb through her math book when we don't even have homework in the class tonight lets me know she is definitely the person we need for Code One.

"Did you see the flyers around the school for the coding club?" I ask. "Me, Chloe, Valentina and Mariama started our own team, and want you to join us. We have to come up with computer code to make our own app."

"A coding club?" Rani tilts her head to the side, and taps her foot for a few seconds. "I don't think I will have the time."

She starts reading her math book again to let me know the case is closed.

"Please, Rani, we need a fifth person," I plead. "And you'd be just perfect. The boys think they are smarter than us, and we want to prove them wrong by beating them with our own all-girls team. Come on, it'll be fun."

She looks up and chews on her fingernail. "I can't fit in another club. I'm in plenty of groups already; the math club, the academic team, and I have Indian dance class two times a week. I don't think my parents would allow me to join anything else, plus I need time to do my studies."

"Hey, Sophie, come on! Mom's pulling up," my little brother Cole shapes his hands like a megaphone and yells at me from across the waiting area. I pretend I don't see him.

"Can you think about it?" I beg again. "The contest is over in three weeks, so you would be able to get back to your other activities full-time after that, and the grand prize is two hundred dollars; forty dollars for each person on the team."

"Forty dollars?" She perks up.

"Yes, if we win, that's what we'll each get."

"Mom's going to be mad if you make her wait!" Cole shouts again through the crowd.

"I gotta go, Rani, what do you say? At least meet us in the computer lab tomorrow during free period for our first coding club meeting and see what you think," I coax. "If it seems like too much, you can bail out."

"Okay." She bobs her head in agreement. "I'll come."

"Great! See you tomorrow!" I rush through the crowd just as Mom's car pulls up. Cole's right, she does get irritated if we make her wait, and I don't want to hear her fussing. I'm thrilled I got Rani to agree to come to the meeting. Code One is on its way!

Chapter 4

Inputs and Outputs, and Loops, Oh My!

I'm so excited about the coding club meeting the next morning that I can barely focus in class. Last night I Googled ways to make different video games and learned about a special language called 'Python' that computer programmers use to code.

"Earth to Sophie." My English teacher, Mr. Bartee, stands by my desk. "May I have your homework?"

"Oh sorry, yes, sir," I mutter, pulling my assignment out of my backpack to turn in.

Across the room, Nathan and Toby look at each other and snicker. *Meanies.*

"Let's start our novel discussion," says Mr. Bartee. "Besides friendship, what is another theme of the book, *Wonder?*"

Please don't call on me. Please don't call on me. I shrink in my seat. I was so busy reading up on coding last night that I didn't finish the chapter.

Nathan raises his hand and answers. "Inner beauty is more important than outer beauty. Even though Julian, the bully, was handsome, he wasn't a very nice person whereas the main character, Auggie, was scary looking on the outside but a good person inside."

"Very insightful, Mr. Jones," our teacher smiles, "sounds like you've been reading ahead."

I shake my head. Of course, Mr. Know-It-All would get it right. Mr. Bartee continues with his lecture about *Wonder*, our English novel for the term. It's a pretty good book, and my mom says we'll watch the movie once I'm finished.

Class seems to drag on as long as it takes Cole to finish his veggies before we can get dessert, but finally the bell rings. I can't wait to get to our first coding club meeting.

"Welcome to the world of coding!" says Mr. Perrier, the club leader. "I'm glad to see so many smiling faces."

I slide into a chair behind one of the computers, and Chloe, Mariama, and Valentina take seats nearby. Rani is not here yet. I hope she shows up.

Including my group and Nathan and Toby's team, twenty-four total kids are in the room. A tall boy wearing bright colored, high top sneakers is sitting near Mr. Know-It-All and Toby, so I guess he's one of their other members, along with Leon Princeton, captain of the math team.

"How many of you are new to computer programming?" asks Mr. Perrier. More than half of us raise our hands. Valentina nudges me, points out Nathan sitting with his hands in his lap and a smug look on his face, and rolls her eyes.

I don't know what I was expecting from the computer teacher, but Mr. Perrier is not it. He looks more like a kid right out of high school or college than a grown-up, with floppy, carrot red hair, freckles, and an orange and white striped tee shirt.

"I remember when I was a newbie to coding." Mr. Perrier clasps his hands and stares in the air, dramatically. "Those days are long past for me, and soon they will be for you too. Follow the teachings in this class, and you'll create way-cool programs and be on your way to having a beyond totally tubular showing in the upcoming coding competition next month!"

"'Totally tubular?" whispers Chloe. "He talks like a surfer dude."

We both jump at a loud clatter in the back of the room. Rani has come in late and stumbled onto a desk.

"Excuse me." She blushes and slides into a seat.

"Today's lesson will be about inputs, outputs, and loops," says Mr. Perrier. "For example, when you eat lunch—an input, you have energy—an output."

"Or if it's Xavier's lunch you could have an output of a belly ache!" jokes Nathan.

"You're getting ahead of me," grins Mr. Perrier. "There are indeed ways to program more than one output for a single input. For example, as this young man suggests, you could show two output results for eating lunch at Xavier: 'A'—increased energy, or 'B'—a bellyache. I've eaten in the cafeteria regularly for the past three years and I can assure you that 'A' is the output I've had most often, except on the days they serve mystery meat."

Kids in the back start to giggle.

"To make sure the basics of input and output are clear to everyone, let's do an example using numbers." Mr. Perrier draws a chart on the board with two columns.

He labels the left side, input and the right side, output. "Let's say I add the number "five" to three different numbers. If I start with the number "one" what will I get?"

"Six," answers the boy with the high tops from Nathan's group.

"If I start with the number "four" what will I get?"

"Nine," responds Rani.

"Awesome, what if I have the number "eleven?" continues Mr. Perrier, drawing the numbers on the chart.

"You'll get sixteen," chimes in Mariama.

"Ugh! This is starting to seem like a math class," groans Chloe.

We spend the next fifteen minutes going over inputs and outputs, and then Mr. Perrier teaches us about loops. "A loop is used to repeat a section of code over and over again," he explains. "For example, if I want to have the computer check the grades of every student in the class I can create a code using loops."

Nathan, Rani and Nathan's newest team member, whose name is J.T. Smith, answer most of Mr. Perrier's questions as he continues the lesson.

"All this talk about loops makes me feel like my head is going round in circles," says Mariama after class is over.

"Yeah, coding is going to be a lot more work than I thought," I reply.

"I think it will be fun," says Rani. "We just have to come up with a good idea for our app. When we were leaving the class, Mr. Perrier told me we'll be using a drag and drop program to make the app, so we won't need to memorize actual code for the contest."

"Does this mean you're joining our team?" I ask.

"Of course," she answers.

"Yay!" I cheer.

I formally introduce her to the other girls. Mariama smiles, and Chloe and Valentina both give her a big hug.

"Welcome to Code One!"

"I'm sure happy you're with us, Rani," says Valentina. "Nathan didn't know what hit him when you answered those last two questions about loops."

"It's good someone knew the answer because I'm still catching on to this," I say.

"I'll bet it will make more sense when Mr. Perrier gets us started on the actual programming games next week on the computer," says Rani. "Let's meet this weekend to come up with our app idea."

"Sure," I respond. "What about getting together at my house?"

"How about a sleepover!" suggests Chloe excitedly.

"That sounds like fun," agrees Valentina.

"Okay, I'll ask my mom," I reply.

Chapter 5

Team Meeting

Mom said yes to the sleepover! I happily text my friends in our group chat that night.

Of course, Cole isn't so excited about our plans.

"Why does Sophie get to have her friends over tomorrow?" he whines. "It's not like it's her birthday or anything."

"We are meeting to organize our computer coding project," I answer. "And believe me, none of my friends want to hang around a little eight-year-old, so we won't be bothering you."

"I am *not* little," Cole retorts, "and I don't want to be around your icky friends, anyway."

"Sophie, stop being so mean to your little brother, and Cole, you cut it out with the whining," says Mom. "You may have a couple of your buddies over for two or three hours, Cole, while Sophie and her friends are planning for their computer project."

"Yippee!" Cole pumps his fist in the air. "I'm going to ask Rhythm and Blu to come play my new video game."

Rhythm and Blu Brown are seven and eight-year-old brothers who live down the street. They used to be Cole's worst enemies, but after they started playing basketball together outside on our goal in the driveway, they've become the best of friends. Rhythm and Blu's parents are divorced, and their father is a musician who travels around the world playing in a band, so they don't see him much.

"Just make sure you and your friends don't bother us, Cole, because we have important work to do," I say.

"Don't worry," he answers. "We'll be having our own fun."

After school, we pull the third row down in Mom's SUV to fit in all my friends. Cole scoots into the back row before we can take our seats.

"Move up with Mom, Big Head," I command. He sticks his tongue out at me and slides out the side door of the vehicle.

"Braaammp!" a sound like a loud cow passing gas explodes as soon as I sit down.

"Ewwww!" exclaim my friends.

"Look what Cole did, Mom!" I shriek, holding up the deflated whoopee cushion he must have sneaked into the back seat.

"Apologize to your sister, young man!" my mother says sternly.

"So-rrrry," Cole answers with a sly little smirk.

"You are soooo gross, Cole! Why'd you do something like that?" I keep arguing.

"I was there first. You should watch where you're sitting." Cole says.

"That's enough, you two. Stop it!" orders Mom. "This vehicle is not moving until I get silence."

Cole and I settle down, and my friends join me in the back of the SUV. They start to chatter away about classes and the coding project to change the subject.

"I feel like a bus driver," my mother laughs. "Don't forget to buckle up your seatbelts."

"Let's take a selfie of our group to remember our first coding club meeting." Valentina whips out her cell phone.

"Say cheese!" she says as we all smile.

"You take so many pictures, it's a wonder there's any storage left on your phone," Cole interrupts from the front seat.

"Cole is bothering us again, Mom," I complain. He turns back around before my mother says anything.

"Where's your bag of clothes, Rani?" I notice she only brought her backpack.

"My father is coming to pick me up at seven o'clock," she says. "I have Indian dance class early in the morning and then practice for the academic team tomorrow afternoon, so he doesn't want me to stay up too late."

"I wish you could be with us longer, but I'm glad you get to come over," I reply.

"Yeah, we need everyone working together to come up with something great," says Mariama. "After school yesterday, my dad showed me some ideas for apps, but none of them looked like something we'd want to use."

"Maybe we should look through the app store to see if there is anything we can copy," says Valentina, scrolling through her phone.

"But I want to come up with something that hasn't been done already," answers Chloe.

Cole shares details of his school day with my mother in the front seat. "I need to bring a new chapter book into school next week for our class book exchange," he says. "We're having a party and everybody will get a new book. I want to get that new one from the *Diary of a Wimpy Kid* series."

"We'll go to the bookstore this weekend," Mom replies.

"Yay!" cheers Cole.

"The only time you've been this excited about shopping is when we went on that trip to Game Shop for a new video game, says Mom. "It's good to see you interested in reading."

As soon as we hit the door, Cole runs to call Rhythm and Blu.

"Come on, guys," I tell my friends. "You can put your things up in my room."

"Watch out, Rani!" I exclaim. She slips and nearly slides backward down the stairs.

"You sure are accident prone," says Mariama, catching her from falling.

"I know," answers Rani. "My family teases me about it all the time. My pediatrician says I am growing quickly and will get more coordinated as I get older."

Once in my room, the girls admire my double bed and goldfish, Goldy. Our dog, Bertram, is outside in the backyard because I wasn't sure if any of them might be scared of him. He's sweet, but he weighs 45 pounds, and likes to jump up on you when he's happy. Sometimes he barks at people he doesn't know too well. Bertram also loves to chew on shoes, and I'm not trying to use any of my coding competition prize money to buy my friends new ones.

"Your room is so pretty," says Valentina, rubbing her hand over my frilly, pink bedspread. "I have to share a bedroom with my little brother, Hector, and he still sleeps with a stinky stuffed dog."

Valentina, her grandma, and her brother Hector were flooded out of their home a few months ago when a huge hurricane hit Houston. They camped out with us in my dad's dental office because we were forced to leave our house too. Hector carried his old, stuffed doll with him the entire time he was with us during the storm. The Martinez family is staying with some friends from their church until repairs are done in their house.

"Snacks are in the kitchen, kids!" my mother calls from downstairs.

We rush downstairs to eat the oven-warm chocolate chip cookies she's placed on the table.

"There are enough for each of you to get three," says Mom.

Cole tries to grab my extra cookie, but I snag it before he can slip it onto his plate.

"Stingy," he says.

"You're just greedy," I answer.

"These cookies are great, Mrs. Washington," says Chloe. "Thanks so much!"

"You're welcome. Your project sounds exciting." She smiles. "I've been wanting Sophie and Cole to get exposure to computer programming, and this coding club sounds like a fun way to learn."

Bertram whines at us through the backdoor window.

"Poor puppy, he wants a snack too," I say, then grab a dog biscuit from the pantry and push it to him through the doggy door.

"I love his curly, black fur," Rani watches him out the window.

Ding Dong! The doorbell rings.

"Rhythm and Blu are here!" says Cole. "We'll be upstairs, Mom."

Chloe gets her fancy pen out and we brainstorm, or come up with ideas for what our app could do.

"What if we create a video game like the one boys are making, only better?" she asks.

"Does anyone know how to play Fortify?" asks Mariama. "I've seen commercials of the game on television, but my parents won't let me get it because it seems too violent. Plus, I don't play video games much anyway."

"My parents strictly forbid video gaming because it wastes valuable study time," says Rani.

"This seems like it will be harder than we thought," says Mariama.

"Come on, guys, we've got to find a way to top what Nathan and Toby are doing," urges Chloe. "I refuse to lose to those boys."

"How are we going to make our game better than theirs is if we don't even know the rules?" asks Valentina.

"I know who can teach us," I say. "Cole."

Chapter 6

Fortify

"I thought you didn't want me and my friends bothering you with your "big girl" project," Cole says when we find him, Rhythm, and Blu upstairs in the game room. "Now you all are getting in the way of our game."

"Come on, Cole," says Chloe. "You've got to help us. We need to learn the rules of Fortify, and everyone knows you are an expert at video games. Sophie brags about you all the time."

Cole looks up from his controller and smiles. Chloe sure knows how to get people to do things she wants.

"It's kind of like paintball, but in a video game," explains Rhythm. "You shoot your enemies so you're the last person left."

"Does Mom know you are playing this, Cole?" I ask. "She doesn't like you to play games with shooting."

"It's just cartoons, Sophie," he says. "There is no blood or anything."

For the next ten minutes, the boys demonstrate how to play Fortify.

"Watch out for that man, Cole," yells Mariama. "He almost got you!"

"Go to the shed," calls Rani, biting her nails. "It looks like you can hide in there."

"Wait! Wait!" says Chloe. "Someone is hiding in that bush in front of the shed!"

Suddenly, the cartoon character dressed like an army sergeant that Cole is controlling disappears. The villain character moves his hips from side to side and sways his arms in front of his body in a victory dance.

"Awww man! He got me!" calls Cole. "I can't ever make it past this level."

"Let's play again!" enthuses Blu.

"Pass me the controller," says Rhythm.

The boys turn back to Fortify and tune us out.

"I see how the game works, but it looks really complicated to make as an app with what little coding we could learn in a couple weeks' time," says Rani. "We may have to come up with another idea."

"Yeah, I can see how this game is fun for the boys to play," I say. "But it doesn't look like something we would think up, so it would seem like we were just copying Nathan's team."

"I agree," says Mariama. "Let's come up with some ideas of our own. Forget making a video game like the boys. What things does everyone like to do?"

"Well, you all know that I love shopping, and, of course, fashion," says Chloe, striking a model's pose.

"Me too," adds Valentina. "And taking pictures is also my hobby. This summer mi abuela is going to let me take a special photography class at the public library."

"I don't shop much, but I am interested in clothes right now too, I guess," says Rani. "My Indian dance troupe is going to perform in a festival in Dallas this summer, and I really want to go. My parents say it costs too much to buy a costume and pay for the bus and hotel, but they told me I can go if I earn some of the money. I've been walking my neighbor's dog after school and doing extra chores around the house too. If we win the coding competition, I'll be even closer to my goal. That's why I signed up to be in Code One."

"What are your dance costumes like?" asks Chloe. "Are they those bright-colored, long dresses that wrap around that I see your mother wear?"

"Yes, something like that," says Rani. "The dresses are called saris."

"I'll bet they are really pretty," I say.

"It looks like most of our group is interested in clothes," says Mariama. "Maybe we could do something with that."

"I've got an idea!" I exclaim. "Let's make a fashion app! People using it could dress up characters in cute clothes that are in style now and also fashions from different places like Mexico,

36

Nigeria, and India. Valentina can take pictures of all the outfits we'd use."

"That sounds like a game I'd like to play!" agrees Chloe.

"I love that idea!" echoes Rani.

We continue brainstorming, and Mariama writes down all our suggestions in a notepad.

"This is going to be great!" says Valentina after we've worked about forty minutes. "I really think we have a chance to win."

Chapter 7

Slice to Meet You

"Pizza's here, kiddos!" Mom calls from downstairs. "Ready to eat?"

The boys beat us to the kitchen. Cole and his friends must really be hungry because I've never seen them willingly stop playing their video games.

"Yummy! Cheese and pepperoni pizza!" shouts Blu.

"Mom! The boys are barely leaving us any!" I exclaim as Cole snatches the last cheesy, extra gooey slice.

"Here's another one." She pulls a pizza pie she was warming out of the oven and sets it on the counter.

We tell my mother our plan for the Code One app.

"That's a fantastic idea!" she says. "It should be interesting to a lot people. You'll really get the judges' attention with that one."

Satisfied that we've picked a topic for our app that could beat Nathan's team, we laugh and talk through dinner.

"I think Nathan's Fortify game will win," says Cole.

"Well, if they play it like you all did they don't stand a chance," jokes Chloe. "I'll bet even I could make it past that level."

"You wouldn't last a minute," counters Blu. "Fortify looks easier to play than it is."

"It did look kind of complicated in the last round," Rani chimes in.

Though she is serious about her school work, Rani is pretty funny. She likes to tell silly jokes as much as Cole.

"What's a dog's favorite type of pizza?" Cole asks.

"Puparoni," guesses Rani.

"Why did the teddy bear say no to dessert?" Rani questions Cole.

"Because she was stuffed," Cole responds.

"Looks like you've met your match in the corny jokes department, Cole," Dad grins as he enters the kitchen.

"Hi, Mr. Washington!" greet Chloe, Valentina, and Mariama.

"Whose birthday is it? And why wasn't I invited?" my father teases as he takes off the white coat he wears in his dental office.

"We're getting things ready for our coding club project, Dad," I respond. "And the girls are sleeping over."

"This is our new teammate, Rani," I introduce her to my father.

"Very nice to meet you, and happy you could join Sophie's team." He smiles as she blushes.

"We have a great idea for our app," adds Chloe.

We fill my father in on the details and continue finishing off the pizza. Cole and Rani keep battling back and forth with their jokes.

"What does a pizza say to introduce itself?" asks Rani.

Cole thinks for a minute. "Slice to meet you!"

"Where do you get all these crazy jokes from?" asks Rhythm.

"I like to check out joke books from the library," explains Rani.

"Me too, and sometimes my grandma gives me joke books as gifts," says Cole.

The doorbell rings.

"That's probably my father," says Rani, "I'd better get my things. He texted me that he would be here soon."

"Awww, man! I wish you could stay longer," says Cole.

"I guess you've finally met a girl that you actually like, Cole," my mother teases.

"See you in school on Monday, Rani." The Code One team members all give her a hug.

"Let's plan to meet in our free period again," suggests Chloe.

"We need to leave too," says Rhythm. "Come on, Blu. Our mother told us not to wear out our welcome."

He grabs his bright red jacket and slips on his turquoise and lime green high-top sneakers. Rhythm's hair is styled in a box cut afro with the tips dyed blond, and both he and his brother have cinnamon brown skin like their father's.

"I agree that you'd better head home before it starts getting dark," says Dad. "But you guys are welcome anytime."

"Thanks, see you Cole," say the boys on their way out.

Rani's father comes in to say hello, but doesn't stay long. "I appreciate you including my daughter in the computer programming project," he says to Mom and Dad. "This will be a wonderful experience for all the children."

"Yes we think so too," says my mother. "and thank you for allowing Rani to participate and visit our home. She's a lovely young lady."

"See you later, Rani!" We wave at her from the door.

"Time to head upstairs guys," I say to my friends.

Now that our work for Code One is done, we can have some more sleepover fun.

Chapter 8

The Prank

"Let's play a prank on Cole," I suggest.

"You love to pick on your little brother, don't you, Sophie?" asks Mariama. I admire her bright red, royal blue, and yellow African print pajamas. Her mother sews and makes her the cutest clothes.

"He's the one who's always messing with me," I answer. "You saw what he did in the car after school, didn't you?"

"Really, I didn't think that whoopee cushion was such a big thing," says Chloe, fanning her toenails with a piece of paper.

We've all had our showers and are sitting on the bed in my room, giving ourselves pedicures. Mom and Dad are setting up a movie for us to watch in the game room, and we'll sleep there with our sleeping bags when it's over.

"I don't know about playing a prank," says Mariama. "We might get into trouble."

"Little Cole is so cute and funny too," says Valentina. "I don't want to hurt him."

"It doesn't have to be anything major," I urge. "We'll just scare him a little."

"Okay, what's the plan?" asks Chloe. I whisper it in her ear and her eyes widen.

"Are you ladies ready for movie time?" My father steps into the doorway, interrupting us. "Your cinema awaits."

"Yay! I love to watch movies," says Valentina. "Come on, guys!"

The smell of popcorn fills the room as we enter. Mom and Dad have set out sleeping bags and pillows and blankets for us, and there are two tubs of buttery kernels on the coffee table.

"There's a cooler with juice boxes here by the wall," says Mom. "Dad and I will be in our room if you need anything, and Cole is already sleeping in his room down the hall. Have fun, girls!"

"I've been wanting to see this one," says Valentina as the movie *The Parent Trap* begins on our flat screen television.

"Yeah, I've heard it was pretty good," I answer.

We giggle as the opening credits of the movie begin.

"Chloe, Valentina, wake up."

It's about two hours later. Mariama and I stayed up until the end of the movie, but our other two friends fell asleep.

"What time is it?" asks Chloe, groggily.

"Eleven o'clock," says Mariama. "You guys missed the best part of the movie. That was so funny when they put the lizard on the Dad's girlfriend's head and it crawled in her mouth!"

"Yick, watching that would give me nightmares," shivers Valentina.

"Trust me, you missed a good one," Mariama replies.

"Come on, guys, it's time for our prank on Cole!" I announce.

"Are you sure about this, Sophie?" asks Chloe.

"What if your parents catch us?" questions Mariama.

"They are probably asleep by now," I reassure my friends. "Dad goes to bed at ten o'clock sharp every night."

"Wait! Let me grab my cell phone to take a picture," says Valentina.

We tiptoe down the hallway to my brother's room, and I gently turn the doorknob and tap open the door.

As I expected, Cole is knocked out, snoring gently in his bed. I'm surprised he's not sucking his thumb anymore. I guess he stopped after I kept teasing him and calling him a baby about it last year. I pull a green rubber snake out of my pajama pocket.

"Where'd you get that thing? It looks real!" whispers Chloe, shrinking back.

"Cole won it at the Spring Fling festival last year and put it on my carpet to scare me a couple months ago," I say. "Now it's payback time!"

I put the fake reptile on the pillow right by his face and have to cover my mouth with my hand to keep from cracking up out loud.

Valentina snaps a picture with her cell phone camera, and we shuffle out of the room.

"Does Cole sleep wild?" asks Chloe. "He might knock the snake off his pillow and not even know it's there."

"He usually doesn't move much," I answer. "Unless he has a nightmare or something and then he gets up and goes in my parents' room. I guess we'll see what happens in the morning."

"What are you ladies up to?" asks my mother as we close the door.

"Oh, hi, Mom," I answer. "We wanted to say goodnight to Cole, but he was already asleep."

"It's almost eleven-thirty, and his normal bedtime is nine, so I guess he would be," Mom answers. "Let's get you four settled down to sleep as well. I don't want your friends' parents upset that I got you too much out of your normal schedules."

"But it's a sleepover, Mom! We should be up."

"It's not summertime and you girls have school Monday morning, so off to bed you go,"

"I'm not even tired. I could stay up all night," I say to my friends as we settle into our sleeping bags.

"Me either," Chloe yawns.

Despite my protests, I start drifting off almost as soon as my head hits my pillow. I smile thinking about the fun we'll have tomorrow when Cole wakes up with that snake on his bed. I can't wait to see his reaction!

Chapter 9

Duct Tape

I have a great dream that night about us beating Nathan and Toby in the coding competition. Chloe and I show our presentation on the huge projection screen in our school's auditorium. Then the audience goes wild as Mariama, Rani, and Valentina take the stage wearing an ivory-colored African gown trimmed in gold, a red, teal and silver Indian sari, and a traditional green, white and red Mexican dress. I stand near our waist-high first place trophy as Mr. Perrier hands Chloe a check that's as wide as our front doormat.

"Well done, young ladies! I knew you could do it," he congratulates us.

The boys slump out of the limelight on the side of the stage, heads bowed.

"You were right, Sophie," says Nathan. "I thought we could beat you, but now I realize how wrong I was."

"We should have trusted in you guys rather than thinking we were better," says Toby.

"Exactly," adds J.T., bowing down to our team. "I'll never underestimate a girl again."

"Three cheers for Code One!" Chloe lifts our winning check in the air.

"Yes!" I try to wave my arm to join in the cheer, but I can't move it.

"Come on, girls, let's take a selfie," says Valentina, pulling her cell phone out of her skirt pocket.

"Wait for me!" I call. I want to catch up with them to get in the picture, but both my arms and legs feel like they are wrapped in twenty pound ankle weights.

I can't move!

"Chloe! Valentina! Mariama! Help!!"

"Sophie, wake up!" says Chloe, shaking my shoulders. "You are screaming. Eating all that popcorn so late at night must have made you have a nightmare."

"My arms are stuck!" I cry.

"What?" asks Valentina. "Wait a minute, guys, look at Sophie's hands!"

My wrists are bound together like a mummy's, and so are my feet.

"Somebody wrapped Sophie up with duct tape!" Mariama exclaims.

"Not somebody…Cole!" I wiggle around like a trapped fish under my sleeping bag covers as my friends cover their laughs.

White duct tape binds both my wrists and my ankles.

"Get some scissors," orders Chloe. "Do you know where any are, Sophie?"

"On the dresser in my room," I answer.

Valentina rushes back with the scissors and starts cutting the tape off me, but first takes a picture with her cell phone.

"If you post that on Instapic..." I warn.

"Lo siento, I mean, I'm sorry, Sophie," giggles Valentia. "You just look so funny."

"Yeah, I've never seen you that mad before," laughs Mariama. "Cole got you good this time."

"Wait until I find him!" I jump up once I'm freed.

"I think you all are even," says Chloe, holding me back. "You've got to admit that putting that snake on his pillow last night wasn't very nice."

I simmer down and start chuckling myself. "I wonder what Cole did when he saw it? I guess he did owe me one."

"What's all this noise up here?" My father peeks his head around the staircase. "Are you young ladies awake? It's almost nine o'clock. Come on downstairs. Your mother says it's time for breakfast."

We pull on our robes and the scent of crispy bacon lures us down the stairs. I wonder what Cole will try next?

Chapter 10

Angry Birds

"This breakfast is delicious, Mrs. Washington," says Mariama, swiping a piece of pancake on her fork through a maple-syrup-filled plate before taking another bite.

"You should taste her blueberry pancakes," says Cole. "They're the best."

He looks innocent as he sips from his glass of orange juice, but we all know what he's been up to. I would tell my mother about the duct tape, but I don't want to get into trouble for putting a rubber snake in Cole's room.

"Nice present you left me this morning, Sophie," says Cole. "I've been looking for it."

"I would have wrapped it," I answer, "but I couldn't find the tape. I guess you used it all."

Cole grins, and then sticks out his tongue.

After we finish eating and get dressed, my friend's parents start arriving.

"Thanks so much for hosting the girls," says Mrs. Thompson, Chloe's mom. "My husband and I were invited out to dinner with one of my partners from work, so this sleepover was right on time."

"So you just wanted to get rid of me, huh?" asks Chloe.

"Never, sweetness. I just didn't want to have to find a sitter at the last minute," laughs her mother, hugging her close.

"Well, the girls are always a delight," says my mother. "All the kids got along very well. We had no drama whatsoever."

Little does she know.

Cole is sitting by the coffee table in the family room, sketching a picture. He is really good in art and paints and draws whenever he isn't playing video games or basketball. Hopefully he isn't hatching up any more mischief.

"See you at school on Monday," say Mariama and Valentina as their parents drive up.

"And don't fight anymore with Cole," whispers Chloe, exiting with her mother.

That's easy for her to say; she doesn't have a pesky little brother.

My friends get in cars with their parents, and I wave from the doorstep.

"Bye, Chloe! Bye, Mariama and Valentina!"

They all wave at me from out their car windows.

"Hasta luego, Sophie!" yells Valentina.

I can't wait until we have our next sleep over! After my friends pull off, I go back in the kitchen with my parents.

"It's a warm and sunny day; why don't you kids go outside?" suggests my father, taking a sip from his coffee cup. "I'm sure Bertram will enjoy the company after being stuck in the backyard alone."

"Sure, Dad. Come on, Cole," I call over to him in the family room area. "Let's go."

"You got me good this morning," I say as soon as we enter the garage.

"So'd you," says Cole. "I almost jumped out of my bed when I saw that snake."

"I was hoping you'd wet your pants," I chuckle.

"Then you'd have had to clean it up or else get in big trouble with Mom and Dad for pranking me," he answers.

"I guess you're right, little brother. Let's call it a truce."

"What's that?" Cole answers.

"It means we're even," I say, putting my hand out to shake his.

He looks my hand over good to make sure I'm not tricking him and then gives it a shake.

Woof! Woof!

Bertram bounces up and down, happy as a puppy in a bone factory to see us.

"Easy, boy!" I laugh as he almost knocks me over jumping up to play.

We play fetch with our dog for about fifteen minutes. "I'm getting tired of this game," says Cole. "Let's take Bertram on a walk."

"Yeah, he'd run and get this tennis ball all day if we let him," I answer.

I grab Bertram's leash from the garage, and we snap it on him and set off.

It is nice walking through the neighborhood with my little brother. The sun is high in the sky, which is filled with fluffy clouds that look like pulled out cotton balls. It's hard to believe they are not solids, but are made of water vapor, a gas. Tall grasses blow in the breeze on the side of the pathway, and I admire the numerous shrubs blooming with vibrant purple flowers.

As we approach a neighborhood waterway, I get nervous. Streams in our Houston area subdivision are connected to the Brazos river, which is filled with fish and alligators. Last year, my family actually saw an eight-foot-alligator during a bike ride, not far from where me and Cole are traveling. Valentina would have loved to have snapped a picture of that.

"Get back here, Bertram!" Cole loses hold of the lease and Bertram rushes off to chase a squirrel a few feet behind us. "Come here, puppy!"

Bertram sniffs for the squirrel near a bush.

Movement startles me when I look toward the path again.

Honk! Honk! Honk!

Two angry ducks are rushing toward me and Cole, feathers flapping. One is white with an orange beak, and the other is black with streaks of white and a reddish beak.

My stomach tightens, and I rush backward toward Bertram.

The larger white duck boldly waddles through the tall grasses, ready to attack.

"Leave my sister alone!" Cole jumps in front of me.

Grrrrrr... Ruff! Bertram stops playing with his squirrel friend and bounds to our defense.

Honk! Honk!

The ducks scatter.

I sidle up to my little brother with a pounding heart. "I wonder why the ducks came after us like that?"

"I don't know, but I'm glad they're gone." Cole grabs my hand and we head back home.

"Those sound like geese, not ducks," says my father after we rush inside and describe the attack. "They were probably protecting a nest of baby geese or eggs."

"Maybe that's why the person who gets tapped on the head in the game, 'Duck, Duck, Goose,' is the one who chases other people," says Cole.

"It could be, Cole," laughs my father, rubbing his curls.

"Well, I'm just happy you kids didn't get hurt," fusses my mother.

"Yeah, I won't be going by that pond anytime soon," I answer.

My parents make us sandwiches for lunch, and we spend the rest of the afternoon relaxing in the family room. Dad and Mom watch a boring show on the Home and Garden network, and Cole and I play Monopoly with Bertram dozing at our feet. I don't complain when I catch Cole sneaking an extra fifty dollar bill out of the bank when he lands on my property, though I do make him put it back.

That was pretty cool how my little brother stood up for me against the angry birds. I'm glad I took my friends' advice and didn't play any more pranks on him this morning. It was fun hanging out with Cole and taking a break from thinking about my Code One project. Though he likes to pick on me sometimes, I guess my little brother does consider me a friend.

Chapter 11

Top Secret

"How's your app coming along, Sophie?" Nathan catches me in the hall Monday morning on my way to my locker before first period class.

"Fine, how is yours?" I say just to be polite. Nathan and I used to talk every day and even have lunch together sometimes with our friends, but we haven't spoken at all since the coding club started, and I'm not sure why he's talking to me now.

"Our project is going great," he brags. "J.T. Smith, whose Dad was in the NBA, and Leon Princeton are on the team with me, Toby and Carlton. This weekend we came up with an awesome design for our game."

"Good for you, Nathan," I answer. We reach my locker and I turn my back on him and start rotating the combination.

"No hard feelings about us not putting you guys on our team, I hope, but we already had everything planned out. We couldn't believe it when J.T. agreed to be on our team right before the coding club meeting. We're so psyched we got him."

I whirl around and face Nathan. "Wait a minute, you mean J.T. wasn't even a part of your team when Chloe and I asked if we could join?"

"W-well, not exactly, but he was on the list of people we wanted to ask," he stammers.

"Was I even on the list at all, Nathan? I thought we were friends."

"We are friends, Sophie. Like I said the other day, I really didn't think you'd be interested. It's not like you are a computer geek or anything, and all Chloe and Valentina talk about is shopping and cell phones."

"Just because they like shopping doesn't mean they aren't smart enough to learn coding. You didn't even give us a chance."

"Look, I'm sorry, Sophie. No hard feelings," Nathan responds. "Maybe I should have thought about you girls when we put the team together. Anyway, it looks like things are working out. You all have your own team, right? And you said you have some good ideas. What kind of app are you making, anyway?"

He glances across the hallway, and I see Toby giving him some kind of hand signal. Nathan pushes his backpack awkwardly between us, and his cell phone hits the floor.

"I'll get it!" we say at the same time.

Nathan and I bump heads as we both bend to pick up the cell phone, but I reach it first. As I hand him back the phone, I notice the red video button blinking.

"What's going on, Nathan? Are you trying to record our conversation?"

He shakes his head and pushes up his glasses. "N-n-o, Sophie, I don't know why that was on. I must have hit it by mistake."

By the other lockers, Toby is pretending to talk to Carlton, but he is still sneaking looks our way. I can't believe this! They are trying to spy on us!!

"There is no way I am telling you what we're doing, Nathan Jones! You are just talking to me to figure out how to beat us."

"What do you mean?" he answers. "We told you what our app is going to be about. Why is yours top secret?"

I grab my backpack and slam my locker shut.

"You'll find out exactly what our app does when we win the coding competition."

"Fat chance of that happening," Nathan responds. "I don't know why I even bothered trying to talk to you."

"I don't either," I say, turning on my heels and heading to homeroom.

The nerve of him! I feel even better about our chances for winning now that the boys have pulled this stunt. They must be nervous about something or else they wouldn't be trying to peep out their opponents.

"Toby tried to sweet talk me into telling him about our app, too," shares Chloe, once Code One gathers to work again during our afternoon free period class.

"Well, don't say anything," says Rani. "The less they know the better."

"Yeah, and we don't need to spy," says Mariama. "Our app will win on its own."

Rani opens her laptop and shows us the drag and drop computer program that we'll be using to make our app with.

"It's like fitting together pieces of a puzzle," she explains.

"Oops! Sorry!" Chloe accidently knocks over a water bottle on the table. The liquid spills over a pile of papers near Rani.

"It's okay. This is just a rough draft of my English paper," Rani says, helping to wipe up the mess with some extra napkins she had in her backpack. "I have another copy saved. I'm just glad that water didn't go on the computer."

We each take turns working with the program so that we'll be one step ahead when we go to our coding club meeting tomorrow.

"I thought coding was really hard at our first class, but this is actually kind of fun," says Chloe, moving blocks around on the screen.

"It's not as difficult because we have this drag and drop program that writes the code for us," explains Mariama. "But it teaches us how things work so we'll understand what is going on better as we learn more."

"Keep learning all you can, guys," I urge. "We *have* to win."

When we first signed up, I felt bad about competing against Nathan. Last year, he seemed like an annoying know-it-all when he kept teasing me during the spelling bee competition, but we became friends after we stood up to a bully together at our school later on. It hurts that he'd keep us off his team and then turn around and try to spy on us. He cares about winning more than our friendship. Until we figure out exactly what the boys are doing, we all agree that our coding project is top secret.

Chapter 12

Miss Bollywood

"Let's go to my house for Code One practice after school," suggests Mariama.

"I'd love to, but I can't," answers Rani. "Today is my Indian dance class."

She accidently bumps me with her backpack and almost sends me falling to the floor.

"Whoa!" I exclaim.

"Excuse me, Sophie," Rani blushes.

"Don't take this the wrong way, Rani," says Chloe, "but I'd never figure you for a dancer."

"Chloe!" I exclaim. "That's not nice."

"It's all right," Rani laughs. "I know I'm clumsy. I've been taking Indian dance classes since I was four, and believe it or not I'm pretty good at it."

"Exactly what do you do in Indian dance class?" asks Mariama. "Is it like jazz or ballet?"

"In the class I'm in now we do Bollywood dancing," explains Rani. "It's sort of a mix between hip hop and jazz, combined with movements from traditional Indian dance and other styles. I take a traditional Indian folk dance class too. My parents are happy I like it because it helps me meet other friends from India and learn about our culture."

"That sounds really cool," I say. "I wish I could see you dancing."

"I have an idea!" says Chloe. "We could take a Code One field trip to Rani's class to look at her dance class. Maybe we could see Indian outfits we want to use in our app."

"We don't dress in our formal costumes during dance practice, just leotards and skirts," says Rani. "But there are pictures in the studio that show fancier things we wear."

"Let's do it!" I say. We text our parents to see if it's okay to join Rani at her dance class after school. My mother agrees since I will be working on my coding project. She usually wants Cole and me to come straight home after school to get started on our homework, unless we have cheer or basketball practice.

Rani's father seems happy to see us when he picks her up in his minivan. "I've spoken with all your parents and it seems you are to do some extra research on your coding project at Rani's dance studio," he says. "I'm certain you will find it very entertaining. Rani is quite the dancer and has been studying at this studio for many years."

"She told us," says Chloe. "Thanks so much for taking us to Rani's class, Mr. Patel."

Before heading to the studio, Rani's father drives us through a fast food restaurant for shakes and fries.

"Don't tell your mother, Rani," he winks, and sips on the strawberry shake he ordered for himself. "I know she already packed a healthy snack for both of us, but I'm sure your friends want something to eat as well."

"What about your diet, Papa?" Rani points at his round belly.

"I'll get back on it tomorrow," he shushes her. "Just enjoy your snack."

"Yes! These French fries are muy delicioso!" smiles Valentina.

Rani's dance studio is in a small building in a strip mall, which surprises me. For some reason, I was expecting it to be a big fancy building.

"You all can watch the class from here." Rani shows us a place where we can sit and see inside the room where she'll be dancing through a large, sound-proof glass. Her father goes to the other side of the room to talk with some parents.

The ladies working in the front of the studio are dressed in regular tee jeans, shirts and skirts, not traditional saris. But, like Rani said, there are framed photos on the wall of various performances that show dancers wearing brightly colored, two-piece crop-top and skirt sets and shimmering dresses trimmed with sequins and jewels. Valentina takes pictures of some of the photos with her camera phone.

"This is going to be neat," says Chloe. "I've seen some Bollywood dancers on TV, but never live."

"We could learn some new dance moves that we might want to add into our cheers," suggests Mariama.

"Good idea," says Valentina, who is our cheer team captain.

About twelve other girls come into the studio and join Rani. Her face lights up as she laughs and talks with them. I can tell this is a place she loves to be.

Finally, the instructor, a petite woman with her hair pulled back into a tight bun, wearing loose black harem pants and a plain white tee shirt, shows up.

"Let's warm up first, girls," she instructs. The girls loosen up with some stretching exercises for about ten minutes and then their routine begins to faster-paced Indian music.

"Wow! Look at Rani go!" gushes Chloe as Rani dips to the floor then hops up and moves side to side in time to the music. She is clearly the leader of the group and stands in the center the of the dance formation.

"She wasn't kidding when she said she was good," declares Mariama. "Rani is the star of the show."

The dance routine reminds me of hip hop and looks like a lot of fun. In addition to the fancy footwork, the girls make precise movements with their arms and hands. Rani is glowing and having such a good time with her friends. I can see why she looks forward to coming to her class.

"That's it for this class," says the teacher after the group has run through their routine several times with a few changes. "Great work, girls. See you next week."

"You were awesome, Rani!" Chloe pats her on the back as she comes out. "I can't believe how great you are in your group."

"Yeah, you should totally try out for the cheerleading squad next year," says Valentina, always looking for ways to improve our team.

"That might be fun," says Rani, smiling in between sips from her water bottle. "If I have the time."

"Did you enjoy the class, girls?" Mr. Patel comes to join us.

"Yes, sir," I answer.

"I took lots of pictures of the costumes in the studio and some of you guys dancing," says Valentina. "This is going to look really cool on our app."

"I can't wait to show Mr. Perrier our ideas tomorrow," I say.

"It's going to be great!" echoes Chloe.

Chapter 13

Back to the Drawing Board

As we expected, Mr. Perrier is all smiles when we tell him our app idea at the coding club the next day.

"Sounds like you've really hit on something young ladies! Go for it!"

Our teacher is not so happy about what the boys are planning.

"I want to see some radical ideas," I hear him telling them. "Redoing a popular video game is a way cool way to learn coding skills, but the judges are looking for something fresh, that's meaningful to you as a team."

Nathan and Toby trudge back to their desks, and they seem to be arguing from the expressions on their faces. They speak quickly to each other and then Carlton shreds a stack of papers they were flipping through and shoves it on the floor.

"I knew it!" I tell my group as we watch the meltdown. "Their team is in trouble."

"That means we are already ahead of the game!" Chloe gives me a high five.

"Well, I say we focus on what is going on with Code One, rather than worry what they're doing," advises Mariama. "Nathan and Toby aren't the only people in the competition, you know."

The three other groups, both made up of a mixture of girls and boys, some of them seventh and eighth graders, take their turns speaking with Mr. Perrier, and head happily back to their desks. We don't have any idea of what they're plans are, and they could beat both our teams.

During the second half of the club meeting, a parent speaker named Mr. Fox, tells us about his job as a computer programmer.

"This is an exciting age in the computer field," he says, "and you kids are learning about coding at just the right time. Best wishes in the coding competition and whatever careers you choose in the future.

Mr. Perrier passes out assignment sheets for us to fill out to make sure we complete all the needed steps for our apps.

"I guess it's back to the drawing board," I hear Nathan telling Toby, J.T., Leon, and Carlton, as we all leave the computer lab.

"Don't worry, I'll ask my dad to help us," says J.T.

"How'd Mr. Perrier like your Fortify idea?" I ask Nathan when we catch up to them in the hallway.

"Cut it, Sophie, I'm sure you heard what was going on," interrupts Toby. "We have to choose something else."

"Well, the teacher absolutely loved our ideas," Chloe flips her curls, "even though one of us has dyslexia and all of us are girls."

"Whatever, Chloe," says Nathan. "I'm not even bothering to get into that with you again."

"Admit it, Nathan," I interject. "You'd have been better off joining up with us instead of adding J.T. and Leon to your team."

"The competition is not over," Nathan answers. "And we still have plenty of time to come up with something that will blow your little project out of the water, so don't sleep on our team."

"Oh, we'll be awake all right and watching you boys cry to your mommies after we beat you silly!" Chloe swerves her neck.

"I'll see you guys in free period tomorrow." Rani exits to avoid the drama.

"Yeah, me too," adds Mariama.

"Come on, Nathan." Toby urges him down the hallway to end the fight.

"I'll work all night if I have to, to make sure we beat those guys," says Chloe.

"They think they are so great, but they don't even have an idea for their project yet, and we've already gotten ours started," I add.

"Now that we have Mr. Perrier's approval, we need to get the artwork together to add on our app," suggests Chloe. "It's good that Valentina is taking pictures, but I think it will look cuter if we have some kind of cartoon characters or something on the app that people playing our game can dress up."

"Maybe we can get Cole to sketch them for us!" I suggest. "He's really great at drawing and even placed in the kid's art contest at the Houston rodeo last year."

"Great idea," Chloe agrees. "Ask him after school."

Chapter 14

America's Next Top Models

"Let me get this straight, you want me to draw all the pictures for your app, so you and your friends can beat Nathan and Toby in the coding club contest and win forty dollars each?" Cole sits with his arms folded in the back seat of the car on the way home. "And what do I get?"

"A chance to have your artwork in a real computer app and you'd be helping me, your only sister."

"If I'm drawing the people that will be wearing the pictures of the clothes, then I want some of the prize money too," he demands.

"Oh, all right, I'll give you five dollars," I say.

"Make it half of what you are getting!"

"Mom!" I complain. "Do you hear what he is saying?"

"Well, your brother will be contributing quite a bit of work if he helps you do the illustrations for the computer app," she answers.

"Okay, what about fifteen dollars?" I counter.

"Deal." He holds out his hand to shake mine.

"We need to have drawings of several girls that users of the app can dress up," I explain. "The clothes will be from many countries, not just America, so make sure you draw different types of girls."

"Maybe he could use you and your friends as models," Mom suggests.

"Great idea!" I exclaim.

"Be still!" Cole has me pose as his first model as soon as we get home.

I stand without moving for over twenty minutes, which feels like an hour.

"Come on, Cole. I have homework to do!" I complain.

"If you want the pictures to be good, then you have to quit wiggling around," he responds.

"Draw the girls in plain tee shirts and shorts so that the people using the apps can easily dress them," Mom advises Cole.

I am amazed at how life-like the drawing looks when my brother is finished. He has made a paper doll image of me.

"Thanks so much, Cole. This is great!" I turn to give him a hug and he squirms away.

"Just make sure you give me all my money once the contest is over."

I am super psyched about this project! Chloe texts in our group chat after I share a photo of the picture of me that Cole drew.

Looks great! adds Rani.

The girls agree that we'll each contribute three dollars to the payout for Cole if we win, since it benefits the entire group, so I won't have to give up a huge chunk of my money.

The next day after school, my friends come over and Cole spends three hours drawing their pictures.

"You move around even more than Sophie did, Chloe," he complains. "You need to be still."

"I thought it would look better if I struck a pose," Chloe says, jutting out her hip.

"That looks crazy," Cole answers. "Now just stand by that chair."

"Can I keep a copy of this to take home?" asks Mariama, smiling at her likeness.

"No, we'll need them to upload on to the Code One app," says Valentina. "Maybe after the project is over."

"You're an awesome artist, Cole!" He blushes as Chloe praises him. Each of the paper doll characters is finished and ready to be uploaded to our app.

"Thanks again, Little Bro!" I pat him on the back.

"I'll go over to Mariama's house tomorrow and get pictures of some African dresses," says Valentina. "I took some pictures of Mexican clothes that my grandma had that weren't ruined when our house flooded."

"We'll also need American clothes," says Chloe. "Maybe we can add our cheer uniforms and some of our regular school and play clothes too."

"You all are playing around with modeling and dress-up more than you are doing computer programming," says Cole.

"You're right, Cole," agrees Rani. "Now that we have all these things taken care of we need to get back to doing the actual programming on the computer to get things working."

Chapter 15

Computer Glitch

"Did you finish setting up the storage area for the characters that will be in the app, Sophie?" Chloe asks.

I feel like rolling my eyes, but don't. Chloe has become a real slave driver since we started on this project. I know we want to win, but she acts like even breathing is taking time away from Code One. Who knew my best friend could be so bossy?

Doing the actual programming of our app is much harder than coming up with the ideas.

"I spent two hours trying to get the pictures of the clothes Valentina took uploaded, and then something crashed, and now I have to do it all again," complains Mariama.

"We'll try it again after school," says Rani, shutting her locker.

Our group is gathering for a quick meet-up before school starts. We have divided up the tasks we need to do to finish up our app. Even if we don't end up winning the coding competition, I'm excited to share our work with the judges and the other teams. Our app idea is so good that I'd want to use it even if I didn't help make it. It'll be fun to dress up the characters Cole drew with Valentina's photos of the beautiful outfits from around the globe.

"Once all this is over, I say we have a huge fiesta," says Valentina. "I'll have my grandma make us her famous tamales and churros as a special treat."

"We'll need them," I grumble. "Since we've started this project we've barely eaten during lunchtime because Chloe always wants to leave early to go work in the library."

"You'll be happy we worked this hard, Sophie, when we win that first-place trophy," Chloe responds. "Beating those boys is going to feel so great!"

As if on cue, Nathan, Toby, Carlton, Leon, and J.T. walk up to us at the lockers.

"What's up, girls?" Toby greets us with a big smile. J.T. holds a fancy looking laptop under his arms.

"Just discussing some finishing touches for our prize-winning computer app," answers Chloe. "How're things going with you guys?"

"Our app is definitely coming in first in the coding competition, so you must be talking about how you'll share your *second* place ribbon," responds Nathan.

"Yeah, right," I answer. "We saw you all limping away from Mr. Perrier's desk the other day when he shot your Fortify idea down."

"After class we went home and came up with something even better that will blow all the other teams out of the water," says Toby.

"And what idea might that be?" asks Mariama.

"You wish you knew," Nathan responds. "We're keeping this hush-hush, just like you girls are doing with your app."

"Fine by me," Chloe answers. "We don't need to know what you are doing to know that we will be the winners next week."

"J.T.'s dad is part owner of a computer company, and J.T.'s been doing programming since he was in diapers," says Toby. "How can you all compete with that?"

"He probably still wears diapers now," I laugh. "so he may not be an expert yet."

"I got your diapers," J.T, angry, speaks up for the first time.

"You girls should give up before you embarrass yourselves," interrupts Nathan. "There's no way you have any hope of topping our app."

The bell for homeroom rings.

"Come on, guys, let's get to class," says Rani. "I'll see you in the computer lab during lunch."

"Okay, see you," I reply, moving away from the drama with the boys.

Though I was grumbling earlier about all the work involved in getting our app to function, I am

84

more than motivated now. I'm tired of those boys acting like they are better than us. We've got to work out all the glitches in our program and shut down Nathan and Toby once and for all.

Chapter 16

Crying Over Spilled Juice

Rani comes home with me after school to help with putting the finishing touches on our app.

"I'll be so glad when this is done," I say as we approach my mom's car. I look in the window and see Cole slumped over crying in the back seat.

"What's wrong with him," I ask my mother.

"That's what I'm trying to figure out," Mom answers. "He came in with a gift box, but won't tell me what's in it. If you don't tell me why you are crying this instant, young man, we're heading in to your teacher for answers," she threatens.

"Hi, Rani," she turns to my friend. "Sorry, I'm so frazzled that I forgot to greet you girls properly."

Rani and I slide into the back seat beside Cole.

"Where did you get that box from, little brother?" I ask.

"Today was our book exchange party," he says, frowning at the gift box like it's full of broccoli.

"You had a party and you're crying?" questions Mom. "What sense does that make? I thought everybody got a new chapter book? Didn't you give that *Diary of a Wimpy Kid* book we brought in Monday? What did you get?"

He holds out a copy of *Charlie and the Chocolate Factory* by Roald Dahl.

"Why, that's a wonderful book, Cole," says Mom gently. "I remember reading it when I was in school and loving it."

"It's too big," he wipes his eyes. "And there are hardly any pictures. I wanted a fun book like the *Diary of a Wimpy Kid.*"

"You are such a baby, Cole," I giggle. "I can't believe you're crying because somebody gave you a book."

"Enough, Sophie," says Mom. "Maybe we can read it together at bedtime," she tells Cole. "There are a couple of popular movies made around this book, too. We can watch one together after we finish, and if you get through this book, I promise we'll get a copy of the *Diary of a Wimpy Kid* book too."

"*Charlie and the Chocolate Factory* is one of my favorite books, Cole," adds Rani. "I'm sure you will like it if you give it a chance. The copy I have at home has lots of pictures in it. I'll let you borrow it so you can see."

Cole calms down, and I roll my eyes. I know I didn't act that babyish in the second grade.

"How was your day, girls?" My mother checks in with me and Rani now that the crisis with my 'book loving' brother is over.

"Pretty good," I answer. "We got more work done on our coding project, and Nathan and Toby say they've come up with an even better idea for theirs but won't tell us what it is."

"We're going to finish up everything this afternoon, so we'll be ready to turn it in to Mr. Perrier," adds Rani.

"Well, you should focus on doing the best job you can on your app rather than besting the other teams," my mother answers.

"I know, but we really want to win, since the boys didn't pick us to be on their team," I respond.

As soon as we get home, Rani and I sit at the kitchen table and start programming. We're still having trouble getting the clothes storage part of the app finished. We have the pictures Cole drew of us on the table. Once we finish the storage area we'll scan in the pictures.

"What about moving this piece over here?" suggests Rani, clicking on the computer mouse.

"That just might work," I answer, looking at the monitor.

A half hour after we start coding, Cole bounds into the room wearing a black, full body suit and face mask.

"Make way for the Black Panther," he snarls.

"Get away, Cole," I say. "You're going to ruin our project."

"I am the most powerful superhero in the universe," Cole says, moving closer.

"I'm warning you, Cole. Back off!" I cry.

88

Cole flexes his arm muscles, slides to the refrigerator and pulls out a carton of grape juice. Then he grabs a plastic cup from the dish drainer rack, pours himself a cup of the juice and takes a sip.

While he puts the juice carton pack in the fridge, Cole sets his half full cup on the table by our work.

"I now have the power of the Black Pan-tha," he says.

Rani cracks up laughing. "Your brother is hilarious!"

She hits her hand on the table, tipping over the cup.

"Oh no!" I shout. "Get a paper towel!!"

I try to move the drawings, but I am too late. The purple liquid spills all over them.

Our project is due in just three days and all our artwork is ruined! We still haven't been able to figure out how to load the pictures of the clothes onto the app either. I feel like blubbering like Cole did earlier after he got a copy of *Charlie and the Chocolate Factory* instead of a *Diary of a Wimpy Kid* book. I blink my lashes to hold back the tears as Rani tries to clean up the pictures with a dish cloth. This can't be happening!

Chapter 17

Losing It

As the juice dries, the paper doll drawings turn lilac.

Rani frantically blots them, and then the paper starts to shred.

I look tearfully at the mess. "Why'd you bring that juice over here, Cole?"

He jumps up and skips to the back door.

"I forgot that Mom wants me to feed Bertram," he says.

"Get back here, Creep!" I yell. "You ruin our Code One project and then run off like it's no biggie?"

"I didn't spill the juice, Rani did," says Cole.

"What is going on in here?" my mother comes in after she hears the ruckus.

"I knocked over grape drink on our Code One drawings," says Rani, her eyes watering.

"There's no way we can have our app working right without those drawings, and the contest deadline is almost here," I cry. "We needed to have the pictures uploaded today! It took a while for

Cole to draw them, and we'd need to get the other girls over here for him to redo them, which could take I don't know how long."

"I'm so sorry, girls!!" says my mother getting a dishtowel to wipe up some of the grape juice spots on the table that we missed. She pats both of us on the back.

"You said the project isn't due for a few days, right? Maybe you can come up with a solution. Why don't you call your other team members and brainstorm?"

Woof! Woof! Bertram barks loudly in the backyard, as Cole runs away from him with his food bowl.

"Be back in a minute, girls," says mom. She goes outside to see what other drama my brother is getting into.

Left alone with Rani, I dial Chloe and Mariama and put them on speaker phone. We aren't able to reach Valentina.

"This is one of your corny jokes, right Rani?" Chloe says, after we explain what happened.

"I'm so sorry guys," Rani says again.

"I can't believe you had a grape drink by all the drawings!" Chloe hisses, as she realizes the disaster is true. "It took us hours to get those done, and you weren't even careful!"

"Maybe I can get Cole to sketch more pictures," I suggest. "Can you come over to my house? He'll probably make us pay him something."

"You can use my portion of the winnings," offers Rani.

"I've got a test tomorrow to study for, and my parents have already been complaining that I've been spending too much time on Code One," say Chloe. "There's no way they will bring me over there today."

"We dropped my mom's car off at the shop for repair after school," says Mariama. "My dad just went somewhere in our other car, so mamma can't drive me to your house."

"We're going to lose the competition now, and it's all my fault!" cries Rani.

The rest of us are quiet.

Then the doorbell rings.

"Rani, your father's here to get you," my mom peeks her head in from the back door.

I still don't say anything, and there is silence on the other end of the phone line.

Rani wipes her tears and shakes her head.

"You guys aren't going to speak to me now?" she says. "I know I should have been more careful, and I feel awful about what happened, but you three are just being mean. Any one of you could have spilled a drink, and I wouldn't treat you this way. Maybe you're better off if I'm not in Code One. I quit!"

She grabs her bag and runs to the living room.

"See you later, Rani," my mother comes back into the kitchen from the backyard. "She's sure in a hurry. Does she have a dance class?"

I can't speak.

I feel more terrible than Cole did after our parents made him give up playing video games for forty days. First juice spills all over our drawings, and now Rani has quit Code One. We're probably going to lose the competition, and even worse, we've lost a friend.

Chapter 18

Valentina to the Rescue

"If Rani's going to be like that, we're better off without her," says Chloe. "I was getting tired of her being so clumsy all the time anyway."

"Now that she's quit, we don't have enough people on our team," I say. "The competition rules say every group needs five members, so we'll have to drop out. There's no way we can replace Rani in three days."

"Remember when you knocked over that water bottle on Rani's English paper in the library, Chloe?" Mariama says. "That accident could have ruined our project, but she was nice about it. She even cleaned up all the mess."

"Yeah, we were too hard on her," I say. "Rani has always been super nice to all of us. I was happy to have her on our team."

Chloe thought about what we said. "You guys are right. We should tell Rani we're sorry. Sometimes I get mad too easy. Rani did us a favor by joining Code One, and she was a big help, even though she did make that one mistake."

"Should we call her?" asks Mariama.

"She was really upset when she left my house," I answer. "I think we should talk to her in person. Let's see what Valentina says."

"Stay on the line," says Mariama. "I'll try her on our other land line phone."

Valentina still isn't answering her cell phone, so we decide that we'll meet at Rani's locker in the morning to get things straight. I get off the phone with my friends and start on my homework.

Twenty minutes later, Cole and my mother come in from outside. He apologizes for messing up my project.

"If I could use my Black Panther powers to fix things I would," he says.

"I know you didn't mean for the juice to spill," I answer. "I'm sorry for getting so mad at you. It's just we wanted to beat the boys so badly."

"You still could win," says Dad, who had walked in the kitchen, and overheard us talking. "The project isn't due yet, is it?"

"We have a couple of days left," I answer. "But now Rani has quit the team because we weren't being nice to her."

"That's why she ran out of here so quickly!" says Mom. "Are you going to call her? Rani is such a sweetie! You girls need to make things right."

"I know, Mom," I answer. "We're going to apologize at our lockers tomorrow."

"Well, make sure you do it," my mother says. "It would be a shame for you to lose a friendship over foolishness."

"Your mother's right," says Dad. "I'm happy you have a competitive spirit, but it's also important for you to value your relationships."

"Yes, sir," I say. I wish I hadn't gotten so angry at Rani earlier. Hopefully we can fix things at school.

"Hey Code One! How are you doing?" Valentina is extra cheerful when we see her the next morning. "Que pasa?"

"What's up and que pasa to you!" says Chloe, showing off her growing Spanish skills. "We were trying to call and text you for hours yesterday. Where were you?"

"I dropped my cell phone and cracked the screen, so mi abuela took me to the computer store to get a new one," she says. "We have it on a warranty plan so it can be replaced if anything happens."

"Thank goodness you have that plan," I say. "I know you would go crazy without your cell phone to take pictures with. You are glued to that thing."

"It's good I am," says Valentina. "because I noticed your message about Cole's drawings. It was too late to call you and say not to worry."

"What! Why not?" asks Chloe.

"You guys know I snap pictures of everything," says Valentina. "I took photos of all Cole's drawings to make into a scrapbook later. They are saved on my phone. We should be able to print them out and use them somehow."

"Whew! That was a close one," I say.

"Thank goodness!" echoes Rani, who must have walked up behind us.

"Rani!" I exclaim.

"We are so happy to see you," says Mariama.

"You are?" Rani asks in surprise.

"Yeah, I'm sorry for how I treated you," says Chloe. "I shouldn't have been so mean. It's just we worked so hard on this, and I hate to have to start over."

"I felt horrible about it," Rani replies softly. "I know it was my fault."

"Well, no one should feel like that if something goes wrong on a project," I say. "We're a team, and we work together. It's one for all and all for one!"

"That's right!" says Chloe. "None of us is perfect, and everyone makes mistakes. There's no need to cry over spilled juice. Please say you'll be on our team again, Rani! We need you, and we're so sorry that we argued."

"I'm sorry too," says Rani. "I felt terrible right after I quit the team, but I didn't know how to take it back."

"Code One wouldn't be the same without you," I say.

"I'm so happy we're not fighting anymore, even though I wasn't here for the argument," says Valentina, raising her hands in the air. "Yay Code One! Come on girls, let's do this!"

We link arms and walk to homeroom.

"I've been seeing some totally awesome shows of creativity," exclaims Mr. Perrier during our coding club meeting that afternoon. "Each team has made epic headway on their projects in a short period of time. Stick with the coding club throughout this school year, and you'll be stoked at all you can accomplish."

Chloe raises her hand. "Excuse me, Mr. Perrier, but were you ever a surfer?"

I cover my mouth and snicker.

"Actually, I have ridden a few waves in my day when I was a college student in California. Why do you ask?" he answers.

"No reason," she giggles.

I am amazed at how much we've learned in our few weeks in the club. I kept playing around with the coding program during our free period, and everything is working. Valentina emailed me files with our paper dolls saved on her phone, so I uploaded them and the pictures of the clothes they'll be dressed in.

"Sweet!" Mr. Perrier exclaims as he passes by my computer station.

Across the room, Nathan and Toby's group are working hard on their project too. "That's what I'm talking about!" Toby exclaims, giving J.T. a high five.

I still wonder what they are doing, but focus on our app to make sure it's the best it can be. By the time the hour for our coding club meeting is over, we have almost everything done.

"We can do the finishing touches after school tomorrow," says Mariama.

"Just make sure we eat our afterschool snacks *before* we start working," says Chloe, smiling at Rani.

"Good idea." she blushes.

After all the excitement from earlier, I'm happy things are coming together for Code One. It will be show time in just one day and it looks like we're almost ready.

Chapter 19

Competition Day

Juggling all our schoolwork while completing our app is tough, but we finally get it done by meeting one last time after school at Mariama's house. Today it's time to turn things in for the coding competition.

"Everything is running perfectly!" Chloe smiles as she clicks through the app on the school library computer. "Code One is game day ready!!"

"I feel like our app is great, but we'll see what the other teams come up with," says Mariama.

"Whatever happens, it's been fun working on this project and getting to know you girls better," Rani adds.

"Thanks for being on our team Rani," says Chloe.

"Vamanos, press the send button, Sophie," urges Valentina. "The official turn in time for the apps is in less than ten minutes."

I click the computer mouse, and my stomach drops as the computer makes a swoosh sound, showing the file is on its way to the judges. Right after I submit the file, I cross my fingers to give us an extra stroke of good luck.

"Finally turning in your coding project?" Nathan leans over the computer behind us. "We had ours in last night. It didn't take us long to get all the kinks out of our program because we have such great team work."

"Good for you, Nathan," says Chloe. "Actually, we didn't have any problems to fix on our app. It's just so fun that we wanted to play on it one more night before we turned it in."

"I guess for someone who thinks shopping is fun anything would be exciting. Best wishes, ladies." Nathan shrugs his shoulders and walks off.

To think he and I were friends.

"Wow, I wish Nathan would simmer down with the competitiveness," says Mariama. "We all want to win, but he is too much."

"I'll be so happy to shut him up when our app takes the prize," says Chloe.

I remember how hard Nathan's father was on him when I beat him in the spelling bee last year. Maybe he is having pressure at home to win in the coding competition too. Whatever his reasons are for being so mean, I wish he'd get over them because all this arguing is getting old.

The rules for the coding competition say that the judges will announce the winners tomorrow before school, so we'll have to wait an school entire day and night to find out whether we placed or not.

After school my mother surprises us by inviting my friends to join us at an ice cream parlor to celebrate.

"Win or lose, I'm proud of you girls for entering the coding competition and creating your very own computer app," she says as we place our orders. I get Rocky Road on a sugar cone and Chloe and Valentina both order cups of mint chocolate chip.

"Birthday Cake, please," says Rani, eyeing the vanilla flavored ice cream with multi-colored sprinkles on top. "I'll take that in a cup too," says Cole.

"Hey, why does Cole get ice cream?" I ask. "He's not part of our coding team."

"This is my present for spending so much time having to look at girls and to draw you, Sophie." He laughs in between bites.

"Funny, little brother," I chuckle. "Thank you for drawing the models for our app. They turned out really cute."

"You're welcome, Big Sis," he says with a smile.

"Will you continue on with the coding club after this is over?" asks Dad after dinner.

"Sure," I answer. "We'll still keep meeting during free period for the rest of the school year. I think they are going to have another competition next year, too."

"We are very happy you took a chance and learned something new," says Mom.

Hope our app crushed it with the judges. Chloe texts me before I turn my phone in for the night to my parents.

Me too. I answer.

Chapter 20

Results

As soon as we get to school the next day, my friends and I hurriedly drop our things off in our lockers and rush to the computer lab.

Nathan, Toby, J.T., Carlton, Leon, and a crowd of other kids stand in front of the door blocking the results sheet, so we can't see who the winners are.

"Who won?" asks Valentina, balancing on her tip toes to get a better view.

"I can't believe this, we were robbed!" Nathan exclaims as he and his team move off to the side.

I have a clear view of the sheet now and scan from the top down to see if Code One got first place.

"I don't see our name," moans Chloe.

"Wait! There it is," points Rani.

The three seventh and eighth grade teams got first through third place, and we tied for honorable mention with Nathan and Toby's team.

"All teams did an awesome job on this project," says Mr. Perrier, coming out of the room. "The judges were really impressed with how much you accomplished in such a limited time. What set the first through third place winners apart was how they incorporated elements in their apps that appealed to both girls and boys. We felt like they'd get more use, whereas the two apps that got honorable mention were both great, but catered more to specific genders, one had things that mostly girls would like and the other had things that mostly boys would like."

Nathan and Toby's app was a basketball game that let users pretend they were NBA players. That actually could be a cool game to play, but some girls, like me, who don't like basketball, probably might not be interested. I guess many boys wouldn't want to play a game about dressing up girl characters either, even though it is a good idea.

"Great job, Nathan." I walk up to him and his team. "Even if you didn't win, surprisingly, I do like your app."

"Yeah, yours looks pretty cool too," he responds. "Can I try it out?"

We take turns playing each other's games while my friends check out the apps from the winners.

"You could add in lady players from the WNBA to your basketball app that girls might like," I suggest.

"I was going to say the same thing about your app," Nathan grins. "Add some boys in, there's no reason that all the characters who get dressed up have to be girls in dresses. You could have Western outfits, sports uniforms, or other costumes that male or female characters could wear."

"Looks like we might have had some different ideas if we had been working together," says Rani.

"Yeah, I wish we had thought about making sure all kinds of people liked our apps when we started," sighs J.T.

"Man, I wanted those new Jordan tennis shoes!" laments Toby. "I guess now I'll have to do some extra chores around the house to get the money for my sneakers."

"There's nothing wrong with working hard," says Mr. Perrier, overhearing. "Keep at coding and you may have a shot at the prize money next year."

"Just make sure you use sense and have us on your team," teases Chloe.

"Definitely," Toby smiles and shows his dimples.

He starts asking her questions about our app, and she doesn't go off on him, and even cracks a small smile.

"ToChlo is back in action," laughs Mariama.

I walk around the computer lab and look at all the other apps as people test them out. The winners are really good and very creative, one team even built their own fantasy world on their app. Though I'm disappointed that we didn't get the prize money, I'm happy that we learned about coding and that we're through fighting with the boys. I'm not sure if I'll stay in the coding club until next year's competition, but I'm glad we started Code

One. It will be interesting to see what project we'll do next.

"Come on, guys, let's get a picture of Code One," calls Valentina. The five of us gather together. "Say cheese!"

"Cheese!" we say with wide smiles.

Dear Reader:

Thank you for reading *Sophie Washington: Code One*. I hope you liked it. If you enjoyed the book, I'd be grateful if you post a short review on Amazon. Your feedback really makes a difference and helps others learn about my books. I appreciate your support!

Tonya

P.S. Please visit my website at www.tonyaduncanellis.com to see cool videos about Sophie and learn about upcoming books (I sometimes give away freebies!). You can also join Sophie's club to get updates about my new book releases and get a **FREE** gift.

Books by
Tonya Duncan Ellis

For information on all Tonya Duncan Ellis books about Sophie and her friends

Check out the following pages!

You'll find:

• Blurbs about the other exciting books in the Sophie Washington series

• Information about Tonya Duncan Ellis

Sophie Washington: Queen of the Bee

Sign up for the spelling bee?

No way!

If there's one thing ten-year-old Texan Sophie Washington is good at, it's spelling. She's earned straight one-hundreds on all her spelling tests to prove it. Her parents want her to compete in the Xavier Academy spelling bee, but Sophie wishes they would buzz off.

Her life in the Houston suburbs is full of adventures, and she doesn't want to slow down the action. Where else can you chase wild hogs out of your yard, ride a bucking sheep or spy an eight-foot-long alligator during a bike ride through the neighborhood? Studying spelling words seems as fun as getting stung by a hornet, in comparison.

That's until her irritating classmate, Nathan Jones, challenges her. There's no way she can let Mr. Know-it-All win. Studying is hard when you have a pesky younger brother and a busy social calendar. Can Sophie ignore the distractions and become Queen of the Bee?

Sophie Washington: The Snitch

There's nothing worse than being a tattletale...

That's what ten-year-old Sophie Washington thinks until she runs into Lanie Mitchell, a new girl at school. Lanie pushes Sophie and her friends around at their lockers and even takes their lunch money.

If they tell, they are scared the other kids in their class will call them snitches and won't be their friends. And when you're in the fifth grade, nothing seems worse than that. Excitement at home keeps Sophie's mind off the trouble with Lanie.

She takes a fishing trip to the Gulf of Mexico with her parents and little brother, Cole, and discovers a mysterious creature in the attic above her room. For a while, Sophie is able to keep her parents from knowing what is going on at school. But Lanie's bullying goes too far, and a classmate gets seriously hurt. Sophie needs to make a decision. Should she stand up to the bully or become a snitch?

Sophie Washington:
Things You Didn't Know
About Sophie

Oh, the tangled web we weave...

Sixth grader Sophie Washington thought she had life figured out when she was younger, but this school year everything changed. She feels like an outsider because she's the only one in her class without a cell phone, and her crush, new kid Toby Johnson, has been calling her best friend Chloe. To fit in, Sophie changes who she is. Her plan to become popular works for a while, and she and Toby start to become friends.

Between the boy drama, Sophie takes a whirlwind class field trip to Austin, Texas, where she visits the state museum, eats Tex-Mex food, and has a wild ride on a kayak. Back at home, Sophie fights off buzzards from her family's roof, dissects frogs in science class, and has fun at her little brother Cole's basketball tournament.

Things get more complicated when Sophie "borrows" a cell phone and gets caught. If her parents make her tell the truth what will her friends think? Turns out Toby has also been hiding something, and Sophie discovers the best way to make true friends is to be yourself.

Sophie Washington: The Gamer

40 Days Without Video Games? Oh No!

Sixth-grader Sophie Washington and her friends are back with an interesting book about having fun with video games while keeping balance. It's almost Easter, and Sophie and her family get ready to start fasts for Lent with their church, where they give up doing something for forty days that may not be good for them. Her parents urge Sophie to stop tattling so much and encourage her second-grade brother, Cole, to give up something he loves most—playing video games. The kids agree to the challenge but how long can they keep it up? Soon after Lent begins, Cole starts sneaking to play his video games. Things start to get out of control when he loses a school electronic tablet he checked out without his parents' permission and comes to his sister for help. Should Sophie break her promise and tattle on him?

Sophie Washington: Hurricane

#Sophie Strong

A hurricane's coming, and eleven-year-old Sophie Washington's typical middle school life in the Houston, Texas suburbs is about to make a major change. One day she's teasing her little brother, Cole, dodging classmate Nathan Jones' wayward science lab frog and complaining about "braggamuffin" cheerleader Valentina Martinez, and the next, she and her family are fleeing for their lives to avoid dangerous flood waters. Finding a place to stay isn't easy during the disaster, and the Washington's get some surprise visitors when they finally do locate shelter. To add to the trouble, three members of the Washington family go missing during the storm, and new friends lose their home. In the middle of it all, Sophie learns to be grateful for what she has and that she is stronger than she ever imagined.

Sophie Washington: Mission: Costa Rica

Welcome to the Jungle

Sixth grader Sophie Washington, her good friends, Chloe and Valentina, and her parents and brother, Cole, are in for a week of adventure when her father signs them up for a spring break mission trip to Costa Rica. Sophie has dreams of lazing on the beach under palm trees, but these are squashed quicker than an underfoot banana once they arrive in the rainforest and are put to work, hauling buckets of water, painting, and cooking. Near the hut they sleep in, the girls fight off wayward iguanas and howler monkeys, and nightly visits from a surprise "guest" make it hard for them to get much rest after their work is done.

A wrong turn in the jungle midway through the week makes Sophie wish she could leave South America and join another classmate who is doing a spring break vacation in Disney World.

Between the daily chores the family has fun times zip lining through the rainforest and taking an exciting river cruise in crocodile-filled waters. Sophie meets new friends during the mission week who show her a different side of life, and by the end of the trip she starts to see Costa Rica as a home away from home.

Sophie Washington: Secret Santa

Santa Claus is Coming to Town

Christmas is three weeks away and a mysterious "Santa" has been mailing presents to sixth grader Sophie Washington. There is no secret Santa gift exchange going on at her school, so she can't imagine who it could be. Sophie's best friends, Chloe, Valentina, and Mariama guess the gift giver is either Nathan Jones or Toby Johnson, two boys in Sophie's class who have liked her in the past, but she's not so sure. While trying to uncover the mystery, Sophie gets into the holiday spirit, making gingerbread houses with her family, helping to decorate her house, and having a hilarious ice skating party with her friends. Snow comes to Houston for the first time in eight years, and the city feels even more like a winter wonderland. Between the fun, Sophie uncovers clues to find her secret Santa and the final reveal is bigger than any package she's opened on Christmas morning. It's a holiday surprise she'll never forget!

About the Author

Tonya Duncan Ellis is author of the Sophie Washington book series which includes: *Queen of the Bee, The Snitch, Things You Didn't Know About Sophie, The Gamer, Hurricane, Mission: Costa Rica, Secret Santa,* and *Code One.* When she's not writing, she enjoys reading, swimming, biking and travel. Tonya lives in Houston, TX with her husband and three children.

Made in the USA
Middletown, DE
18 November 2020